First American Edition 2016
Kane Miller, A Division of EDC Publishing

Text, design and illustrations copyright © Lemonfizz Media 2010
First published by Scholastic Australia Pty Limited in 2010
This edition published under license from Scholastic Australia Pty
Limited on behalf of Lemonfizz Media

For information contact:
Kane Miller, A Division of EDC Publishing
P.O. Box 470663
Tulsa, OK 74147-0663
www.kanemiller.com
www.edcpub.com
www.usbornebooksandmore.com

Library of Congress Control Number: 2015953930

Printed and bound in the United States of America
1 2 3 4 5 6 7 8 9 10

ISBN: 978-1-61067-508-6

MAKING WAVES

Kane Miller
A DIVISION OF EDC PUBLISHING

The dolphin Squirt was named by
Hannah Moses
and
Rachael Ewins

FOR HENRIETTA

Chapter · 1

"On your marks. Get set. Go!" shouted the swim coach.

Emma Jacks dived into the pool and began to swim as fast as she possibly could. Taking a breath only every third stroke, Emma moved her arms quickly and strongly and kicked her legs as hard as she could. As she turned her head from side to side, she glanced at the other swimmers to check where she was in the race. Emma could tell from the swimsuits they wore who the other swimmers were. Hannah, one of her best friends, wore a navy-blue swimsuit and was just a little bit behind on her left. Nema, definitely not one of her best friends, was just in front on her right wearing a bright-pink swimsuit with silver stars.

Emma kept swimming, kicking even though she thought her legs were going to fall off. She was catching up to Nema and, while she wouldn't have enough time to beat her, she would be close. As they came up to the end of the pool, Emma stretched out her arm and slapped it only a split-second after Nema.

"A great race, girls, that was a really close finish," cried Ms. Tenga, one of their teachers and the race timekeeper.

Emma was relieved and pleased with her race. Holding on to the lane rope, she looked around to see how everyone else had done. Nema had come first, she had come second and, yes, Hannah was third and Isi, another really good friend, was fourth. Her other good friend, Elle, was just finishing, struggling with slow, heavy strokes, in last place. Elle put her head up and took a huge gasp as she touched the end of the pool.

"Way to go, Ellesabelle!" cried Isi.

"Thanks, Is," said Elle, smiling in an exhausted kind of way, "but even you couldn't get excited about me coming last."

"But you finished this time," Isi pointed out.

"That's true," said Elle, climbing out of the pool. "Go, me."

Smiling, Emma climbed out of the water after her friend. She knew Elle wouldn't be upset about coming last in the race: swimming just wasn't Elle's thing. Running, however, was a different matter. Elle normally picked up all the blue ribbons at field day. She ran fast, she jumped high and long. Elle was just better on land. But Emma, Hannah and Isi all loved the water and they were strong swimmers. They were hoping their times would be good enough to get them on the relay team for the upcoming swim meet. How much fun would it be to race together?

"Well, it seems we have our relay team for the meet," said Ms. Tenga, looking up from her clipboard. "Isi, Hannah, Emma and, with the fastest time, Nema. Good job, girls. Now quickly, off to the locker rooms please."

"Thanks, Ms. Tenga," said Nema, "but I actually think I was pretty slow that time. I am sure I can be a lot faster."

"Aaaargh!" groaned Hannah, burying her head in her towel as the girls headed to the locker room. "That is so, so, so…" Hannah seemed lost for words.

"So Nema?" suggested Emma.

"Exactly," said Hannah. "I know she is a good swimmer, but she thinks she is so much better than everyone else. And how does she manage to flick her hair even when it's wet?"

Nema was a good swimmer, a really good swimmer. She trained hard and she swam for a team outside of school. Everyone knew that because Nema would bring her huge swim team bag to school, even on days when there wasn't swimming, and show people her name sewn in big letters across the bag. It was pretty cool, as were all the different colored swimsuits Nema had. Everyone had to admit that Nema was a great swimmer, but did she have to boast about it all the time?

It seemed she did.

Now that the tryouts were over, everyone rushed to get changed and then filed onto the bus to return to school. Emma sat next to Hannah, and Isi and Elle sat across the aisle from them. Nema sat behind them, by herself because her swim team bag took up most of the other seat. As usual, she had carefully positioned her bag so her name was clearly on display.

"Okay, everyone, may I have your attention please," called Ms. Tenga. She stopped speaking and waited until everyone had stopped talking. "Strong swimming today, I am really pleased with how much effort everyone put in. As you know, the swim meet is next week. What you don't know, and this is exciting, is that the meet won't be at our normal pool. It will be at a much larger one, an Olympic-sized one, with great diving blocks at the deep end. It will be a fantastic experience."

Emma put her hand up. "Ms. Tenga, how deep is the deep end?"

"Pretty deep, certainly much deeper than our normal pool, and there's a diving pool, which is even deeper. We're lucky to be going there. If you're all good, I might even let you do some cannonballs in the diving pool at the end of the meet."

Isi squealed, as she normally did when she was excited, which was quite often, but this time so did Hannah. Even Nema smiled. Emma, however, bit her lip.

Hannah, who noticed these kinds of things, glanced at her friend. "What's wrong, Em?" she asked.

"You're not letting Nema get you down, are you?" asked Isi, leaning across. "I mean, we're on the team too. Even Nema won't be able to take all the credit for a relay."

"No, it's not Nema, it's nothing really," said Emma. "I just didn't realize we would be at a new pool for the swim meet."

"I know," cried Isi, "and how fun will it be if we can do cannonballs!"

"What's the matter, Emma?" asked Nema, but not in a voice that made you think she was the slightest bit interested or concerned. "You're not still afraid of the deep end, are you? Only little kids are afraid of the deep end. Babies."

Someone at the back of the bus laughed.

Emma's face went bright red. How could Nema tell that secret?

Emma and Nema had used to be friends, quite good friends, and even nearly best friends for a while. They had gone to the same kindergarten and started at the same elementary school together. They went to each other's birthday parties and played at each other's houses after school. Like all friends, they talked, a lot, and sometimes they told each other secrets. It was sort of a game, like Truth or Dare, and, one time, Emma had to tell the truth about the things she was scared of. It took a little while. Emma was scared of a lot of things then: spiders, her brother's skeleton mask, the dark, the creepy-looking house at the end of their street and deep water.

Even though she loved swimming and loved the water, Emma didn't like being in over her head, in water where she couldn't touch the bottom. Even when she was swimming in a pool her imagination would start telling her that there were things lying on the bottom, things waiting to grab her legs and pull her down. It didn't help that her older brother Bob thought it was hilarious to call, "Shark!" just as she dived into a pool. She knew, obviously, that there wasn't a shark in her local swimming pool, but it didn't stop her scrambling out, just to check, just to be sure. She knew it was silly, ridiculous actually, but that didn't help. Her fear didn't stop her swimming, it just made her a bit nervous. And, that day back in first grade, during that game of Truth or Dare, Emma had told Nema about her fear of deep water. She then forgot all about it. After all, friends don't tell secrets, do they?

That was ages ago, years ago, in fact. Now Emma and Nema weren't really friends anymore. Emma thought Nema had changed: she had stopped wanting to play games and started wanting to talk about hairstyles and TV stars. She stopped playing soccer at lunchtime and started flicking her hair a lot. And she started being mean to people. No one was exactly sure why, but everyone was sure it wasn't nice. Nema would make fun of people. She seemed to sense when people were feeling a little unsure, but rather than make them feel better, she would make them feel worse. Like the time she had teased Elle about her new glasses. Elle actually looked pretty cool in them, but they were new and they embarrassed her. Nema seemed to know that and made fun of her anyway. It was just mean. Emma couldn't stand people being mean to anyone, but she especially couldn't stand it when they were mean to her friends. She had learned to stand up to Nema, but she still found it hard. There were times when it just seemed too hard, when Nema seemed too mean. Now, when Nema had blurted out her secret fear in front of everyone, was one of those times.

Emma could feel a sort of burning sensation on her skin, a heat spreading from her neck to her face. She knew her face was turning red. She turned her head and looked out the bus window. She could feel her eyes prickling, but she blinked them tight—there was no way she was going to cry on the school bus, in front of everyone.

Hannah put her hand on her friend's knee and gave it a little squeeze just as Nema called out again.

"Sorry, Emmy, I couldn't hear you," Nema cried. "Did you say you *are* still afraid of the deep end?"

This time some other girls behind Nema laughed.

Emma blinked her eyes tightly again and clenched her fists. *Why does Nema do this?* she thought. *I have to answer her. I can't let Nema think I am upset, even if I am!*

Emma took a deep breath. "No," she said, but the word came out so softly that for a moment she wasn't even sure she'd said it.

"I'm sorry," said Nema, again in a voice you knew meant she wasn't sorry at all, "I still can't hear you."

"She said no, Nema," shouted Hannah. "Haven't you got some hair to brush?"

Emma smiled a little at that and Nema stopped, but it was too late. The damage was done. Everyone would think Emma was a scaredy-cat baby.

"Well," continued Hannah, in a voice the whole bus could hear, "I'm scared of puppets."

The bus went silent, that is until Nema started speaking again.

"OMG!" she exclaimed. "Are you all babies? How can you be scared of *puppets*?"

"I saw a bit of this really scary movie my sister was watching," said Hannah, to no one in particular, in a voice the whole bus could hear. "There were these wooden puppets with mouths that moved and they all came alive and started stalking humans. I know it's silly and it was only a movie, but now when I look at puppets, they still freak me out."

"I know!" called out someone else from the back

of the bus. "Those puppets are sooooo creepy! It makes you wonder about all your other toys too."

"Do you think our old Barbies might turn on us?" cried another girl, laughing.

Emma gave Hannah a grateful look. Her friend had taken all the attention away from what Nema had said and now the whole bus was talking about freaky puppets and other toys coming alive. That was such a Han thing to do. She was a good friend; *she* wouldn't ever tell a secret.

Emma and Hannah had also been at kindergarten together and had stayed friends all the way through elementary school. In many ways, they were the opposites of each other: Emma had long, light hair, Hannah's was short and dark; Emma had blue-green eyes, Hannah's were brown; Emma was quite tall, Hannah was shorter; Emma loved dogs, Hannah was a cat person. But in lots of other ways they were like twins: they both liked gymnastics and swimming, they were both good at art and math, and they both loved animals and chocolate—but, then again, who didn't love chocolate? Together with Isi and Elle, they formed a little group of friends who liked doing the same things and looked out for each other. Just like now.

"Oh no," said Emma, smiling. "Now I think I am scared of puppets too!"

They all laughed and Emma didn't feel quite so silly anymore. *But*, she thought to herself, *I did used to be scared of the deep end and I can still get nervous about deep water if I think about it. And me, a secret agent!*

Being a secret agent was Emma's much bigger secret and it was something she had definitely never told Nema about. When she wasn't Emma Jacks, swimmer nervous about deep water, newly scared of puppets, lover of animals and best buddy to Hannah, Isi and Elle, she was Special Agent EJ12, code-cracker and field agent in the under-twelve division of the **SHINE** agency.

And Emma didn't know it yet, but Nema wasn't the only one making waves. Evil agency *SHADOW* was also up to no good somewhere in the ocean and they would have to be stopped. **SHINE**

wouldn't pick an agent who was nervous about deep water for an ocean mission.

Would they?

Chapter •2

SHINE was a top secret, international spy agency. Its agents worked to foil the plans of evildoers all over the world, particularly those of *SHADOW*, a secret agency that would stop at nothing to make money—and to try to stop SHINE stopping them. *SHADOW* agents had tried to build satellite dishes in a beautiful and protected rain forest, they had tried to melt the Antarctic ice cap to sell bottled water and were always trying to steal the inventions of SHINE's scientists. There seemed little that *SHADOW* would not do to get what it wanted and at a time when most people were trying to make the world better, *SHADOW* seemed determined to make it worse.

Luckily there was SHINE. But before they could stop *SHADOW*'s evil plans, SHINE had to find out what those plans were. SHINE did this by intercepting the messages that *SHADOW* agents sent to each other. *SHADOW* sent messages on email, on mobile phones, on pieces of paper, carved into trees, even in the words of songs. To make things more difficult, these messages were in code. Not only did SHINE have to find the messages, they then needed to crack the codes. That was where agents like EJ12 came in.

At school, Emma liked math. You knew where you were with math—it didn't change on you. Even if you didn't understand a math problem immediately, you knew that if you worked your way through it there would be an answer, just one answer. Math was reliable and Emma liked reliable. Which is why she also liked codes. If you looked carefully, you could always find a pattern and once you found it, you could crack the code. Even really hard codes always had a key, you just had to look for it. And, as EJ12, Emma was good at code-cracking. She was also pretty good at the missions that followed. SHINE had a motto: "If you crack the code, you take the load." That meant the code-cracking agent then went on the mission and EJ had been on lots: she had swung through rain forests on vines, jumped over rope bridges, gone down caves and snowboarded as she tracked down and stopped SHADOW agents. EJ12 always seemed to keep her cool and overcome her fears when she was on a mission. Which, when she thought about it, was a little weird. As EJ12, she was can-do, will-do, but as Emma Jacks, she was more, "don't think I can do." Why was that?

The bus pulled up to the curb back at school and everyone piled off noisily. It was lunchtime and the kids were starving after a morning of swimming tryouts. Most of the girls, at least the ones with long hair, headed straight for the girls' bathroom to dry their hair on the hand dryers.

Piinngg!

That was Emma's phone. Even though it was turned off for school, it was ringing. That was because it was no ordinary phone; it was a SHINE special-issue phone, a cross between a game console and a touch screen phone. It was the best phone a girl could have, although for Emma any phone was the best phone a girl could have as her parents had said she was too young to have one. She only had it because when the phone came as part of her SHINE agent welcome pack, Emma's mom, herself a former SHINE agent, had to agree to let her keep it—after all, what secret agent didn't have a phone?

The phone had lots of normal apps, but there were also secret ones that agents could access with a special pin code. There were code-cracking apps, voice-changing apps, animal ID apps, a camera with

X-ray zoom and secret listening devices. **SHINE** also used the phone to send mission alerts to their agents. They sent alerts when they needed them to access the **SHINE** Mission Tube and report to HQ for a mission briefing. That special alert was the *Piinngg!* Emma had just heard and her Mission Tube agent access point was the last stall on the right in the girls' bathroom at her school.

The girls' bathroom where she was already heading. That was good.

The girls' bathroom, where every other girl in her class seemed to be heading as well. That was bad.

As Emma pushed the door open, she could see that there were lots of girls already inside. There were girls everywhere. Girls crowding around the hand dryers trying to dry their hair, girls in the stalls, girls at the sinks, girls just hanging around.

Gee whizz, lemonfizz! This is hopeless, thought Emma. *How am I going to get to the stall and, even if I do, how will I be able to access the Mission Tube with all these people here?*

She wouldn't be able to. There was nothing for it, Emma would have to wait. She just hoped she wouldn't have to wait all lunchtime. **SHINE** liked their agents to report promptly and they timed them. Just as Emma was starting to think the girls were going to stay in the bathroom forever, Ms. Tenga came in. That was unusual because the teachers hardly ever came into the girls' bathroom.

"Come on, girls," she cried. "I am sure we don't need everyone in here and I am also sure everyone's hair is dry now. Now, quick as you can, finish what you are doing and out, everyone out."

Girls started to shuffle out to the playground.

"Not you, Emma Jacks," said Ms. Tenga.

Did Ms. Tenga just wink at me? thought Emma. *I think she did.*

"Emma, please stay and make sure there is no trash left anywhere and that everything is shiny and clean. That would be a great help, thank you. Right, everyone else, out!"

Did Ms. Tenga just say "shiny and clean"? wondered Emma. *Was that a coincidence?* Emma thought back to other times where Ms. Tenga seemed to be in the right place at the right time to help her. *Hmmm.* Emma didn't have time to think about that now though. Even if it was just a coincidence, Emma was grateful: she now had the girls' bathroom to herself and she needed to work fast.

Quickly, before anyone else came in, Emma ran to the last stall on the right, pushed the door open and locked it behind her. She put down the toilet seat, sat down and opened the toilet paper holder. Hidden on the side, where no one would ever notice, was an electronic socket. Emma took out her phone and inserted it into the socket, just like a phone charger, and waited. There was a beep. Emma entered her pin code and took her phone out of the socket. There was another beep and then a familiar message flashed up on her phone screen.

> WELCOME BACK EJI2.
> HOLD ON!

EJ clutched the sides of the toilet and held tight as the wall behind the toilet started to move. It spun around, with toilet and EJ attached. Once it had spun all the way around, EJ slid off the toilet and onto a beanbag (**SHINE** liked their agents to be comfortable) at the top of what looked like a giant slide. This was the **SHINE** Mission Tube, a system of underground tunnels that whizzed agents into and around the **SHINE** network. The wall then spun back and EJ could hear the click as the stall door unlocked on the other side. That would ensure no one became suspicious about a locked door and an empty cubicle. **SHINE** thought about these details. EJ waited while a protective shield clicked into place over the beanbag and then took her phone and keyed in "GO." And go she did.

WHOOOOOOOOOSH!

EJ loved lots of things about being a **SHINE** agent. She loved the places she traveled to, she loved the gadgets she used, she loved the animals she encountered on missions and she loved going down the Mission Tube. Whizzing around corners at high speed, it was like a carnival ride that just went on and on, more than making up for having to start the mission in the bathroom.

Finally the tube straightened and leveled out as EJ came to a stop at a small platform with a keypad. She had arrived outside the Code Room. Again she keyed in her pin code and waited, this time for the security check to commence. To ensure that there was no unauthorized access to the code rooms, SHINE changed their checks daily—there had been head scans and singing tests, eye scans and signature checks. EJ wondered what today's check would be. A tray with a small glass of water and a bowl came out from under the keypad and EJ heard a digital voice.

"Gargle water and spit into the bowl. Please be accurate," said the voice.

"Ew! That's gross!" said EJ, but she did as she was instructed.

She took the glass of water and drank it. Rather

than swallowing, EJ swirled the water around and around in her mouth and then tipped her head back and gargled.

GUUUURRRRGGGGLLLLE

EJ then took the small bowl and held it up to her mouth. Carefully she spat the water out again into the bowl and put the bowl back on the tray.

The bowl slid back under the keypad. For a moment nothing happened.

Did I not spit enough back in? wondered EJ. But then she heard a beep.

"A little messy but agent DNA and identity confirmed. Please drop in, Agent EJ12!"

There was then one final beep, the floor under the beanbag fell away and EJ dropped down, beanbag and all, into a chamber underneath the Mission Tube. EJ had entered the **SHINE** Code Room. It was sparsely furnished, just a chair and a table and a clear plastic tube sticking out from the ceiling above the table.

EJ heard a whizzing sound. She put her phone

on the desk and put her hands out under the tube, catching the capsule that then popped out. Inside the tube were a piece of paper and a pen. EJ read the message on the paper.

> For the eyes of EJ12 only.
>
> (Message intercepted from SHADOW 11.15. Sent to EJ12 11.17. Urgent decode required.)
>
> BLACK HARVEST 1 COMPLETE
>
> A-SUB WORKS A TREAT
>
> NOW BEGIN TO TEST
>
> LUCKY I AM BEST

EJ looked hard at the code, studying the writing, if you could call it that. She was pretty sure they were letters, but what had been done to them? This was not going to be an easy code and she was already way behind on time because it had taken so long to get everyone out of the bathroom.

EJ's head started to rush and her thoughts whirled around and around as she began to tap the pencil on the table. None of these things were good for code-cracking.

Calm down, she told herself, *you need to look at codes slowly. There is always a clue somewhere. The code is broken up into parts, so just look at the first part.*

BꞭACK

EJ looked again, this time slowly looking at each letter of the coded word.

The fourth letter is a C, thought EJ. *But why does it look normal and the others don't? But, actually, some of the others don't look that weird after all—the B and the K just look a bit funny, sort of upside down.*

And then EJ noticed that some of the code was reflected on her phone screen. The reflection picked up some of the words on the paper, but now, when she looked at them on her screen, they looked completely normal. *A mirror code,* she thought. *Can it be that simple?*

EJ took her phone and switched to mirror app, then held the screen over the message, taking one line at a time. She wrote down what was reflected in the mirror.

BLACK   HARVEST   1   COMPLETE
BLACK HARVEST 1 COMPLETE

A-SUB   WORKS   A   TREAT
A-SUB WORKS A TREAT

NOW   BEGIN   TO   TEST
NOW BEGIN TO TEST

LUCKY   I   AM   BEST
LUCKY I AM BEST

She then wrote the message out again.

BLACK HARVEST 1 COMPLETE

A-SUB WORKS A TREAT

NOW BEGIN TO TEST

LUCKY I AM BEST

It's like a poem, thought EJ, *but a bad poem, a really bad poem.* And then it struck her—there was only one person in *SHADOW* who used really bad poems. Adriana. Adriana X, brilliant but crazy *SHADOW* scientist—and evil twin sister of the head of **SHINE**, A1. EJ scrawled a note under the decoded message.

I think this is from Adriana X.

Then she rolled the paper back up and popped it up into the tube. Immediately it was sucked away to the Operations Room where A1 would be waiting for it.

I'd better get there too, thought EJ, as she re-entered the Mission Tube. *A1 is not going to be happy.*

Chapter • 3

A1 did indeed not look happy, but her face brightened as EJ came through the large automatic doors from the Mission Tube to the **SHINE** Operations Room.

"Welcome back, EJ12," said A1. "You took a little longer than usual. Any problems?"

"It wasn't the code," explained EJ, blushing and anxious that A1 might think she was losing her touch as a code-cracker. "It was more the problem of getting all the girls out of the bathroom. I thought I would be waiting forever, but then one of the teachers, Ms. Tenga …"

EJ stopped for a moment. She had just realized something about Ms. Tenga's name. If you mixed the letters up you could spell a-g-e-n-t, agent. There were too many coincidences. Maybe she should ask A1 about...

"Yes," said A1. "Do you have something to ask me?"

"Was that a coincidence, A1?"

"Was what a coincidence, EJ12?" said A1.

"Ms. Tenga..."

"Ms. Tenga?" repeated A1.

"This may sound silly, A1, but is Ms. Tenga a SHINE agent too?"

A1 smiled. "Yes, she is, EJ," she replied. "I wondered how long it would take you to figure it out. We have found it useful to cluster agents together. You never know when they might be able to help each other. I'm glad she could help you today. And now we need your help, EJ12. Let's take a look at your decoded message." And with that, A1 looked up and spoke loudly and clearly. "Light Screen, lower."

On A1's command, an enormous screen came down from the ceiling. It was the Light Screen, a giant, voice-activated plasma screen that accessed the Internet, all SHINE's classified files and databases, radio and television channels and GPS technology. It also linked in with SHINE's research and surveillance stations all over the world. EJ's decoded message flashed onto the screen.

For EJ12's Eyes Only

(Message intercepted from SHADOW 11.15. Sent to EJ12 11.17. Decoded message received at SHINE 11.34. Time taken to decode 4.00.)

BLACK HARVEST 1 COMPLETE

A-SUB WORKS A TREAT

NOW BEGIN TO TEST

LUCKY I AM BEST

"Good work, EJ," said A1, "and I think you are right, this message has all the signs of being from my sister, Adriana."

"But what is she doing?" asked EJ. "What is 'black harvest'?"

"We think it is something to do with this," replied A1, passing EJ a small plastic container with a long black stick inside. "It accompanied the message."

"It's a stick?" asked EJ.

"Sort of," replied A1. "An underwater stick anyway. It's a piece of coral, black coral to be exact and the skeleton of black coral to be even more exact. The tissue of the coral is brilliantly colored, but the skeleton is this distinctive black. It is quite beautiful, isn't it?"

"Yes, but what does this have to do with Adriana and *SHADOW*?" said EJ.

"We weren't sure until you decoded this message, but now I think we can piece a few more bits of the puzzle together. We think this coral is the 'black harvest' mentioned in the message. We think Adriana is harvesting black coral. We have been monitoring some unusual changes in the levels of water pollution up in the reefs of the marine heritage area off the northeastern part of Australia and coral harvesting may explain it."

"But why would Adriana want black coral?"

"Black coral is quite rare and extremely valuable because it mainly grows deep in the ocean, deeper than where most divers can go. It is difficult to get large quantities of it and that makes it very expensive. However, we believe that Adriana has devised a new way to get the black coral. And lots of it. If she has, it could be devastating for the whole of the reef system. Our leading marine scientist can help us here." A1 turned to the Light Screen. "Teleconference Professor Agent F15H."

An image of a young woman with short black hair appeared in the corner of the Light Screen.

"Hello, A1, Agent EJ12."

"Thanks for joining us, F15H. Can you please give us some background on the reef system on the northeastern coast of Australia and some of the changes you have been monitoring?"

"Yes, of course. Let's look at the area on the 3-D map."

A map appeared on a part of the Light Screen, a satellite, 3-D photomap. It started with Earth as a globe sitting in space. EJ could see the white of Antarctica and then above that the browny green of the landmasses of Australia and New Zealand, both surrounded by water. Hugging the right-hand side of the top bit of Australia was a thick line of dark among the blue.

"Is that the Great Barrier Reef?" asked EJ12.

"It is indeed, well done," said F15H. "You can just make out the spread of islands that lie off the coast. But let's go in closer. Map, zoom Australia, northeastern coast."

The map zoomed in closer and EJ could now see different shades of blue in the ocean, the whites of the waves and the craggy browns and greens of mountains on the land. It was an incredibly detailed map. EJ could even see the waves moving.

"Now we can see the reef better," said A1.

"It's enormous," said EJ. "I didn't realize that it

was so long."

"The Great Barrier Reef is the longest stretch of reef in the world," said F15H. "It's millions of years old and home to thousands of ocean species. We can look at pictures and footage that can give you an idea of the richness of life under the water. Light Screen, zoom. Show images."

The Light Screen was suddenly awash with images. Photos flashed and video streamed, showing fish, big and tiny, in all the colors of the rainbow. EJ watched as more images appeared on the screen. There were pictures of dolphins diving, whales swimming and sea turtles gliding through the blue-green water. And there was coral, in all shapes, sizes and colors—browns, oranges, pinks and purples, blues and reds. Some of the coral looked like flowers, some like mushrooms, some like bushes and trees and some looked just weird, like nothing EJ had ever seen before. And, swimming over and through it all, were hundreds, maybe thousands, of fish. It was hard to take in just how many weird and beautiful species there were living together under the water.

"That's awesome!" said EJ12.

"Yes, and for once, I am pleased to say, that word is used correctly," said A1 smiling.

EJ grinned back, a little embarrassed. A1 sounded just like her mom, who was always carrying on about how you couldn't describe a TV show as awesome.

"It is," agreed F15H, "but it is also under threat. Climate change is altering the balance of the sea water and making it too acidic for many of the species. We are starting to see disturbing signs of the smallest species being affected and if the smallest species are affected, soon all the other species will be too."

EJ scrunched her nose and narrowed her eyes, feeling a bit confused.

F15H glanced down at her from the Light Screen. "Let me explain," she said. "Everything in nature is connected. If something happens to one part it has an effect on something else and then that thing will affect something else and so on. Take tiny plankton," she said. "Light Screen, show plankton."

An image appeared of tiny and transparent insect-like things swarming in the water like little sea bugs.

"These organisms, many of them microscopic, are probably the most important group of species in the ocean," said F15H.

"They are? You're kidding me!" exclaimed EJ. "They are so small. What about fish, dolphins and whales?"

"Of course they are all important, but without plankton, all of those creatures run into trouble," continued F15H. "Plankton is the food of many larger animals. If there is a problem with the plankton there will be a problem with the fish, with the whales and, slowly, the balance is upset, the food chain collapses and the reef and all the life that depends on it begins to die."

"Is Adriana doing something to the plankton?" asked EJ, biting her lip anxiously.

"Probably. If she is harvesting the coral, that will definitely be increasing the pollution levels of the water as well as causing other damage to the reef. For the last month we have been seeing some much higher than expected pollutant levels in particular areas of the reef, but we can't find the cause. There are also areas where the reef has been completely destroyed. Light Screen, show images."

Now more photos spilled onto the Light Screen, but these were not beautiful, they were awful. There were images of water so clouded with dirt you could hardly see anything, images of lifeless coral smashed and dried on the seabed. And there wasn't a fish to be seen.

"This is the same reef?" asked EJ, shocked.

"I'm afraid so, at least a part of it," replied F15H glumly. "We believe that this is where the piece of black coral sent with the message came from."

Suddenly, there was a beep. F15H looked down and checked her pager.

"Will you excuse me, A1?" she said. "We have just had some more test results in and I need to look at them."

"Of course," replied A1. "Many thanks, Agent

F15H, and please keep me informed. **SHINE** out."

The image of Agent F15H disappeared from the screen.

"So, EJ," said A1, "we are pretty sure that Adriana is harvesting black coral. And Adriana's message says 'Black Harvest 1 complete.' That must mean she plans to carry out more."

"We have to stop her!" declared EJ.

"Yes, but first we have to find her," said A1. "And, so far, we have found no trace of her."

"Maybe that's because of the A-Sub," suggested EJ. "The message says 'A-Sub works a treat.' Perhaps she says that because no one can find her?"

"I think you are right, EJ," replied A1. "We think Adriana's A-Sub uses some kind of secret stealth technology that allows her to travel underwater without detection. But now that we know a bit more about what we are looking for, we have a few secrets of our own that might just help us find her."

"We do?" asked EJ.

"Yes," said A1, "but we haven't got much time. We need to get you to the reef, find Adriana and stop her before her harvesting and testing does any more damage."

EJ wondered if now would be a good time to tell A1 about her secret.

Chapter • 4

Somehow A1 already knew. Indeed, A1 seemed to know a lot of things EJ didn't expect her to and she often seemed to know what EJ was thinking, which could be disconcerting. Sometimes, however, it could also be comforting. This was one of those times.

"EJ, you will be fine. You just need to take the plunge and dive right into the mission. Once you get started you won't even think about things you used to be scared of."

EJ wasn't so sure, but she was determined to

stop Adriana doing any more damage to the reef. Somehow that now seemed scarier than the deep water.

"So," continued A1, "let's commence your mission briefing. You did very well in your pool dives so you are ready for ocean diving. And in case you were worrying, Agent Captain C2C will be there to show you the ropes. You will remember C2C, our lead ocean agent, from your Antarctica mission and, if I remember correctly, one of our training camps. You will meet C2C at our secret diving station."

"I didn't know we had a secret diving station," said EJ.

"Well it wouldn't be very secret if you did," said A1, smiling. "Now, we must keep moving. Your wetsuit is waiting for you in the dressing room. Please change now while I get your equipment ready."

EJ headed off to the dressing room at the end of the Operations Room. Inside the middle cubicle, hanging up on a hook, was a yellow one-piece swimsuit and a black-and-purple wetsuit with the

SHINE logo across the front. On the floor was a pair of rubber dive shoes. EJ quickly changed out of her uniform into the swimsuit and picked up the thick, spongy rubber wetsuit. It was tricky to put on: EJ started by putting one foot into the leg and gradually rolling the wetsuit up. It was a bit like putting on tights in the winter. Eventually, after quite a bit of yanking and stretching, EJ managed to get the wetsuit on. She pulled the cord at the back to bring up the zip, slipped on her dive shoes and she was ready. She folded her uniform and left it in the paper bag marked "**SHINE** home delivery." Her clothes would be washed and returned to her mom. **SHINE** knew how to look after the details. EJ walked, rather awkwardly, out of the dressing room and back to the briefing table where A1 was standing.

"It looks like a good fit, EJ," said A1. "And have you noticed anything about your dive shoes?"

EJ looked down at her shoes. They looked pretty normal to her. She looked back up at A1, a little confused.

"You may recall our **SHINE**-issue mission boots?"

EJ certainly did. The **SHINE** mission boots looked like normal hiking boots, but when you clicked the heels they could change into ice skates, jumping coils, even a water scooter. The only problem was that they were a little unreliable: you never knew what would come out first.

"The old mission boots had a few development issues," said A1, once again seeming to read EJ's mind, "so we have streamlined things a bit. These dive shoes only do two things, dive shoes and…"

EJ had clicked her shoes and flippers appeared.

"Flippers!" she cried.

"Exactly," said A1 with a smile. "Now, let's continue. Here is a waterproof case for your **SHINE** phone so you can still use all the apps underwater. You can clip it to your wetsuit, and here are your mission charms. I assume you are wearing your bracelet."

EJ was. All **SHINE** agents were issued with a bracelet that could carry a large number of charms. These, however, were no ordinary charms, they were actually CHARMs, Clever Hidden Accessories with Release Mechanism and they used a technology invented by **SHINE** scientists that shrunk equipment and gadgets to the size of a charm. The item could be returned to its original shape and size and be ready for use with a simple twist. It was ingenious; an agent could be fully equipped for a mission, all on her wrist, and no one would ever know. EJ did wonder how her charm bracelet would work underwater though.

"All **SHINE** charms are completely waterproof and tested to work at even a thousand meters depth," said A1.

How does she do that? thought EJ.

"I just do. I think you will like these charms," continued A1. "You saw one of them at a recent training camp."

Please let it be the dolphin charm, please let it be the dolphin charm, chanted EJ to herself.

"The first one," began A1, "is the dolphin charm."

EJ accidentally let out a little shriek of excitement.

"EJ12, is everything all right?" asked A1, turning to face EJ and looking concerned.

"Yes. I'm sorry," said EJ, her face reddening. "Go on, A1."

"Thank you, EJ12. This is the dolphin trainer charm that Agent IQ400 showed you. It allows agents to work with dolphins by communicating with basic commands. We have been secretly training a small pod of bottlenose dolphins near our diving station."

"Training them to do what, A1?" asked EJ.

"To search," replied A1. "Dolphins have built-in sonar that allows them to explore their surroundings. The dolphins send out noises and the noises hit things in the water and then bounce back to the dolphins, allowing them to understand what those objects are. It is a very sophisticated system, much cleverer than anything we have been able to invent. Most importantly, they can recognize new things, things that have been introduced into the sea. For dolphins this ability helps keep them safe. For us it means we can find things that people put into the sea. Things that perhaps shouldn't be there."

"That is so clever," cried EJ.

"Yes," agreed A1, "and by working with the dolphins, by rewarding them with their favorite fish, we have been able to train them to show us how to find those things."

"Like Adriana's A-Sub?" said EJ.

"Let's hope so," replied A1. "Adriana doesn't know we are using dolphins so she may not have designed the A-Sub to avoid detection by them. Agent C2C will brief you on how to use the charm at the dive station. The next two charms are similar to the penguin charm you already have." A1 held out two charms, one in the shape of a sea turtle, the other a butterfly fish. "These charms are animal feeding charms. The turtle charm will release a bag of sponges, sea turtles' favorite food, and the butterfly fish charm releases a universal fish food." Finally, A1 gave EJ a charm that looked a little like a plastic bottle.

"A water bottle?" asked EJ.

"In a way," replied A1. "This is a test flask, the

first in a new range of charms IQ400 has been developing. As you know, **SHINE** already has a large range of spy charms, tools and gadgets that help our agents on missions, but now we also have sci charms that can help us with research and testing."

"Spy charms and sci charms, I like that," said EJ.

"I rather thought you might. I do too," said A1, smiling. "I am very excited about these charms, EJ. They will allow our agents to help carry out important scientific and environmental research all over the world. Let me show you how this one works."

A1 twisted the charm and waited. A small clear plastic bottle with a thin neck and wide base appeared.

"Now, this may look like an ordinary flask but it isn't, thanks to microchip and transmitter technology embedded in the plastic. It is a smart flask. The agent collects a sample—some coral, sand or seawater perhaps—and the flask will test the sample and send the results directly to the **SHINE** laboratory where they can analyze it and respond as necessary. Remember, EJ, whatever Adriana is up to, she is changing the balance of the water and we believe this imbalance will be stronger the closer you get to her and her activities. We need you to take water samples while you are up there. You can carry out the test by scooping up water yourself, but the flask also fits perfectly into the robotic arm fitted on *SHINEmobile 3.*"

"*SHINEmobile 3*?" asked EJ. She remembered *SHINEmobile 3* from her Antarctic mission. It was a cross between a jet ski that went on water and a snowmobile that traveled on ice. It was like riding a very fast scooter and it was very fun. *But SHINEmobile 3 can't go under the water, can it?* EJ thought.

"Yes, EJ," said A1, "The new and improved *SHINEmobile 3* is now fully submersible. It will be your own personal submarine, complete with robotic tools for underwater work."

"Wow," gasped EJ, "that is so cool!"

"And it is waiting for you on board *SHINEforce 10* along with Agent LP30, who will fly you to your drop point. The reef is in deep trouble, EJ12. We have to find Adriana and stop her secret operation before it is too late."

EJ put on her charms, clipped her phone to her suit and took a deep breath as she headed for the door. She was starting to feel a little out of her depth.

Chapter • 5

"Welcome aboard *SHINEforce 10*, EJ12," said LP30, turning away from the plane's controls to smile at EJ as she came aboard. "I like the wetsuit. I'll get us up in the air and then brief you on the new features of *SHINEmobile 3*. But now, strap yourself in and prepare for takeoff."

The engines of *SHINEforce 10* surged in power and its wheels began to roll. It quickly picked up speed as the plane powered down the runway and then lifted into the air. In no time they were up high in the sky. LP30's voice came over the speakers.

"Okay, EJ, we are now cruising comfortably, but don't get too comfortable. **SHINE***force 10* has been upgraded for supersonic capacity; it will be a short flight. We need to review your pre-mission checklist. Correct gear?"

"Check, wetsuit on. Dive shoes on."

"Mission charms attached?"

EJ double-checked her bracelet. "Check."

"Confirm mission objectives."

"Locate Adriana and A-Sub and prevent coral harvest."

"That's affirmative, EJ12," replied LP30. "We are already flying over the water. If you look out on your right side you will be able to see the beginning of the reef."

EJ looked out the window. As on the photomap, she could see the way the coral reef stretched up along the coast like a ragged shadow under the water. The Great Barrier Reef was not one reef but lots of reefs forming a long line. As the jet began to descend, EJ could see that the sea wasn't just one uniform blue but lots of different blues. There was the dark, dark blue of the deep ocean, then the light blue of the shallower areas dotted with the white tips of the waves. From the plane, the reefs looked almost black. Then EJ saw something she couldn't believe: a large heart in the middle of the ocean. She quickly realized it was a patch of reef shaped like a big love heart.

"Is that real?" cried EJ to LP30.

"The heart?" said LP30, without turning around. "It's real."

"Is it natural or man-made?"

"Completely natural. Isn't it amazing?"

It was indeed and as EJ looked out over the reef, she kept wondering why anyone would want to destroy it. But Adriana was doing just that and she was down there somewhere.

"We are approaching the drop-off point, EJ," shouted LP30. "You need to get into *SHINEmobile 3* and prepare for air launch."

"Air launch," repeated EJ. "It can fly as well?"

"Glide, actually," answered LP30. "There is a new hang gliding feature. *SHINEmobile 3* is stored at the back of the jet, just behind the door. Please take your position in *SHINEmobile 3* and give me the thumbs-up when you're ready to go."

EJ unstrapped her seat belt, got out of her seat and opened the door at the back of the cabin. It led to a small area that was like the trunk of the airplane. In the middle was a purple vehicle that looked like a cross between a jet ski and a mini submarine. It was the new *SHINEmobile 3*.

EJ put on the helmet and life jacket that were hanging over the handlebars, climbed onto the seat and strapped on the seat belt. She locked her phone into the socket on the jet ski dashboard and gave LP30, who was looking back from the cockpit, the thumbs-up.

"Okay, EJ, I am about to open the back of the jet. When I do, release the break and press the G button on your dashboard to activate the glider. Once out of the plane you can steer down to the sea. As you approach the water, press the J button and *SHINEmobile 3* will convert to jet ski mode and you can ride to the diving station to meet

Agent C2C. Your phone will automatically activate the satellite navigation system—the location of the diving station is already uploaded to your phone. Ready to go?"

"Check," said EJ12. She was excited. She had parachuted out of planes before and loved it, but this should be even better.

"Okay, doors opening, you are ready for drop. Good luck, EJ12!"

The back of the jet slid open and a rush of cold air filled the plane. EJ released the brake and pressed the G button. Two sail-like wings shot out from each side of the vehicle and it started to move. As it rolled out of the plane, EJ felt the *SHINEmobile 3* drop but, before she had time to worry that it was going to keep dropping, its wings caught the wind and EJ felt the vehicle pick up again. EJ turned the handlebars and, pointing the nose slightly downward, she began to glide down toward the ocean. It felt so light, as if she was flying in a paper airplane. She circled, spiraling her way down, and the water came closer and closer. EJ hit the J button and her glider converted to jet ski mode. Perfect timing.

And a perfect landing.

EJ looked around. There was nothing but water. When she looked to the horizon, there was just one long, wide expanse of sea with sunlight dancing on the sea's surface, making it sparkle. EJ looked down. From the plane, the water had looked deep blue, but up close, it was more blue green, aqua even. *That makes sense,* thought EJ. *Aqua, water, I suppose that's why that color is called that.* EJ liked it when words worked that way. What she didn't like however, was that she couldn't see the bottom of the ocean. The sea must be deep, very deep.

Okay, she thought to herself. *I am not even going to think about what's underneath me. I need to get to the diving station.*

EJ turned on the GPS. The station was about

five nautical miles away. *I'd better get going,* she thought, as she started the engine and slowly pulled back on the accelerator. There was a whirr as the electric motor kicked in. With only a small jolt, EJ was off, speeding across the water.

From the air, the water might have looked smooth, but there were small waves everywhere. EJ gripped the handlebars as the jet ski was thrown up against the waves and then crashed down again. THWACK, THUMP, wave after wave after wave. It was hard work but fun at the same time.

EJ felt the wind and salt water whip around her face. She checked the GPS. She should be approaching the diving station, but EJ couldn't see anything but water. She rode along for a little farther and her GPS began to beep.

I must be close, thought EJ, as she slowed the jet ski and came to a stop. *But there's nothing here, only a whole lot of seaweed.*

The jet ski floated a bit farther along, the GPS beeped even more loudly and EJ felt a jolt as the jet ski seemed to bump into something. *But what?*

What have I hit? she wondered. *There's only seaweed and seaweed isn't hard.*

Beeeeep!

Maybe the GPS is broken, EJ thought. It was then that she saw that another text screen was flashing on the dashboard of her jet ski. She read the message.

AT LOCATION
PRESS UP FOR LIFT

Lift? wondered EJ, but she checked the dashboard and saw there was an UP and a DOWN button. She pressed the UP one. There was a gushing noise and then bubbles began to appear. The seaweed floating on the surface began to move as it was pushed up into the air. EJ watched in disbelief as slowly an inflatable dive pontoon, complete with a small cabin covered with seaweed, rose up from the water.

Well, thought EJ, impressed, *A1 did say it was secret.*

EJ could also see another **SHINE**mobile tied to a pole at the far end of the pontoon. It had been pulled up with the pontoon. *That must be C2C's jet ski,* thought EJ. *But where is C2C?*

Just as EJ was about to climb onto the pontoon, there was a loud splash behind her. She jumped up in her seat and spun around to look. There was nothing there. EJ turned back to the pontoon.

Then there was another splash. EJ turned around, quicker this time, but again she saw nothing. She was beginning to feel just a little spooked.

Seconds later there was a third splash. EJ looked back again and this time, she thought she saw something black moving up and down in the water. She kept looking and, yes, there was something and whatever it was, it was coming closer. EJ froze for a moment, holding the handlebars of the jet ski tight, her knuckles whitening. She wasn't even in the water yet and she was scared.

SPLASH!

There it was again, another splash and then a large blowing sound, as if something, or someone, was pushing out air.

Someone was. Right next to EJ's jet ski, a head popped up, a head wearing a mask and a yellow snorkel—with a **SHINE** logo on the side.

"EJ12, it's good to see you again. It's me, Agent C2C."

EJ hoped she didn't look as embarrassed as she felt.

Chapter •6

"Well, I see you found the **SHINE** dive station," said C2C, who had now climbed up onto the pontoon and removed her dive tanks, mask and snorkel. "A small, water-powered lift system allows us to keep the pontoon hidden in the water. It would stick out like a sore thumb in the middle of the ocean so we keep it submerged whenever possible. We are not far from the reef and I was just doing a quick check while I waited for you, but there's no sign of any unusual activity here. What is the latest intelligence from HQ?"

EJ got off her jet ski and joined C2C on the pontoon.

"We know Adriana is working in something she is calling an A-Sub and that she has completed her first harvest of black coral somewhere not too far from here," said EJ. "But our radar tracking systems can't seem to find any trace of her."

"We'll find her," replied C2C, "but first we need to get you marine-mission ready. Your scuba gear is in the dive cabin. Put it on and we can start."

"Start what?" asked EJ slightly nervously.

"Your first ocean dive," said C2C. "What a treat awaits you!"

EJ didn't see it quite that way. "I thought I'd just use my **SHINE**mobile," she replied.

"Most of the time you can," agreed C2C, "but there may be times when you need to dive. This exercise will prepare you for that and you must be feeling hot in that wetsuit. A swim will cool you off."

EJ had to agree she did felt pretty uncomfortable. The rubber suit felt hot and sticky. She opened the cabin door and found the gear. Remembering her training, she strapped on her oxygen tank and checked the gauges. She took her mask and attached her snorkel before clicking her dive shoes together to turn them into flippers. She had all her gear and she was ready. She just didn't feel ready.

"Come on, take the plunge," cried C2C, who was already back in the water. "There's nothing to be afraid of."

"Are you sure?" said EJ, thinking there might actually be plenty to be afraid of. "How deep is it here?"

"Not so deep at all," replied C2C. "And once we are on the reef it will be less deep, it is like a platform in the water."

A little reassured, EJ dropped into the water. The wetsuit that had felt tight and clammy was now almost impossible to feel at all. It was like a second skin. EJ dunked her head to wet her hair and put on her mask.

"You remember how to use your scuba gear?" checked C2C. "Just breathe normally through your mouthpiece, go down slowly and check your air supply regularly. When you come up, go slowly as well. Right, down we go."

And before EJ could say, "I think I might stay here for a while," C2C had pressed the Down button for the pontoon. She slipped under the water and began to swim away. EJ had no choice but to swim after her. At first she paddled with her head above the water, but then she put her head under the surface and kicked off with her flippers. She slid through the water and a trail of tiny bubbles streamed from her scuba gear as she breathed.

EJ soon adjusted to breathing underwater with the scuba gear. All her practice dives in the **SHINE** training pool had paid off. What took a little longer to get used to was the silence all around her. The only thing she could hear was her own breathing and the sound of the bubbles. It was as if she had entered a different, silent world where she was the only noisy one. There was nothing to hear. There was also not much to look at, only sand, murky water and some brown seaweed waving at the bottom. EJ felt a little disappointed. It was not at all like the pictures on the Light Screen.

Then, in the distance, a shape seemed to be forming, something dark and round against the green-blue sea. EJ stiffened slightly and watched. As the shape came closer, she could make out two things slowly rising and falling, like wings, from its sides. It was swimming right at C2C and EJ.

EJ squealed, but with excitement not fear as she realized what was coming toward her. The round thing was a sea turtle, a large wrinkly-necked sea turtle, gliding effortlessly through the water with just the occasional flap of its flippers. It came within three feet of EJ, looked straight at her with its large, old-looking eyes and then began to chew on EJ's flippers. EJ was amused but also confused as to what to do next.

C2C gestured to EJ, shaking her charm bracelet.

Of course, thought EJ, *feed it so it stops feeding on my flipper!* She took her turtle charm and twisted it. In seconds she was holding a bag of sponges. EJ took one out and deactivated the charm. She then held a sponge out to the sea turtle. It immediately let go of EJ's flipper and took the sponge right out of her hand and swam away.

EJ gave C2C the thumbs-up and they swam on, following the turtle, until they came to a reef.

EJ was entranced. She had seen pictures of the ocean underwater on the Light Screen, on TV, even in 3-D at the movies, but nothing prepared her for what she was seeing, what she was in, now.

The seabed was transformed from sand to an underwater flower bed, bursting, overflowing with brightly colored coral. There was round coral, spiky coral, wavy coral, coral that looked like cabbage, coral that looked like little trees and coral that didn't look like anything EJ had ever seen before. And the colors were amazing: yellows, orange, blues, reds and purples even more vivid than on the Light Screen. And everywhere, simply everywhere, there were fish. Small fish, big fish, fish in schools and fish swimming solo. There were whirlpools of tiny silver fish that moved as one, swooping and darting in and out of the reef. There were larger fish: bright blue with vibrant yellow fins, zebra-striped fish, orange-and-white-striped fish, blue fish with yellow tails, green fish with yellow eyes. EJ took out her phone and activated the animal app and fish pictures and names flashed on her screen: now she knew there were clown fish wriggling in sea anemones, angel fish feeding on sponges and brightly colored butterfly fish dashing from coral to coral.

EJ watched in wonder as the fish swam through the shafts of sunlight that dappled the reef, as if they were crossing a busy intersection, going about their business. She saw sea sponges and starfish and, then, incredibly, a seahorse floating with its tiny almost transparent fins fluttering and its long snout moving up and down. EJ watched as it whirred its way between long, waving strands of seaweed. It was magical.

She was so absorbed by what she was watching that EJ completely forgot she was on a mission until, swimming just above a coral bed, she spied something that didn't belong there. She signaled to C2C and then dived down to pick it up. It was an underwater video camera. But whose camera was it and what had it filmed? EJ and C2C swam quickly back to the pontoon to find out.

Their heavy oxygen tanks beside them, EJ and C2C sat on the pontoon of the dive station and replayed the footage on the camera EJ had found.

"I think this was taken in much deeper water," said C2C. "You can see it's darker."

"Yes, and that's black coral," said EJ. "I recognize it from the images F15H showed me. It only grows in deep water. Look, there is masses of it, it's like a field. I wonder if this is where Adriana plans to harvest." EJ zoomed in. "And see here, on the seabed, C2C," she continued, thinking there were rather a lot of Cs, seas and sees for one sentence, "there are small metal disks with flashing lights running along in a line by the coral."

"They're some kind of marker," said C2C, looking closely. "But what are they marking? The harvest area?"

The camera screen went black. There was no more footage. EJ turned the camera around, examining it closely. Then she saw it, in small writing on the bottom of the camera: "Aqua-Cam—Another brilliant AX creation for *SHADOW* Inc."

"It's Adriana's camera!" she said. "She must have dropped it while she was looking for beds of black coral and laying her markers. If we can find the markers, maybe we can find Adriana. But how will we be able to find those small markers in all this ocean?"

C2C smiled. "With a little bit of help from **SHINE**'s secret underwater weapon. I think A1 mentioned it and now you can meet it, or should I say, her. Squirt can find those markers."

"Who?" said EJ.

"Squirt."

"Pardon?"

"Squirt, your mission buddy. She's a dolphin."

EJ smiled. She loved being a secret agent.

Chapter · 7

"**SHINE** has been working with dolphins for some time now, training them to help search for things in the ocean," explained C2C. "Dolphins have a natural sonar system that allows them to locate objects in the water. They find things better than any device we could ever invent and they are naturally curious. They are excellent search agents, just like our sniffer dogs on land. And Squirt is one of the best agents in our marine mammal division."

"So a dolphin can help me find Adriana and her A-Sub?" asked EJ.

"Exactly," said Agent C2C. "Now activate your dolphin charm and call in your buddy."

EJ didn't need to be asked twice. She took the dolphin charm and twisted it. It transformed into a small black box with a **SHINE** logo on it. There were two buttons labeled Return and Search.

"We can't really talk to dolphins," continued C2C, "but we have been successful in teaching them basic commands. This device sends out the commands with a noise the dolphins have learned."

"Why do they come?" asked EJ.

"Because they are curious," said C2C, "and because we have their favorite fish. Mainly because of the fish."

"We have fish?"

"Oh yes. Inside the dive cabin you'll find a cooler that holds large buckets of fish. You'll need to have fish with you when you work with Squirt. Every time she does what you ask her to, you must reward her. There is also a small pouch so you can carry the fish while you are diving."

EJ went over to the dive cabin and returned with

a big white bucket. She was holding it as far away from herself as she could.

"Oh, I forgot to warn you," said C2C, laughing, "they smell a bit! Now let's see if Squirt is around. Push the Return button, EJ."

EJ pushed and could just make out a high-pitched squeal.

Weeeiiieiiiieiiiiiiii

She pushed the button again.

Weeeiiieiiiieiiiiiiii

EJ waited and watched, her eyes scanning the ocean, but she couldn't see anything. She kept looking, scrunching her eyes as if somehow that would help her see better, and craning her neck. Then she thought she saw something. Just a little wave? No it wasn't, it was darker, more definite in shape. It was a fin, and suddenly a dolphin leapt out of the water, high into the sky, before diving back into the ocean. EJ was delighted.

"There she is!" cried EJ. "She's so, so beautiful, so graceful! Look, she's jumping again. Look, she's coming over!"

"Why don't you go in and meet her?" asked C2C. "But be careful, EJ, don't touch Squirt and don't flap your flippers. Dolphins take that as a sign of aggression. But do take the fish and you'll soon be friends."

EJ couldn't believe how lucky she was—she was going to meet a dolphin! Completely forgetting to worry about the deep water, she strapped on the fish pouch and filled it with the small fish from the bucket. She then lifted on her tanks again, pulled her mask over her head and put her snorkel in her mouth. EJ dropped down into the water and looked in the direction where she had last seen the dolphin leaping.

EJ heard Squirt long before she saw her. In an otherwise silent ocean, she first heard a series of clicking noises and then some whistles and then more clicks. And then, just feet away, she saw her, a bottlenose dolphin. She was much bigger than EJ thought she would be, twice, nearly three times EJ's size, but there was something about her face that made EJ feel safe, even happy. She squealed with excitement. The dolphin seemed to look right at her and then let out another whistle sound before leaping out of the water and diving back in again. EJ squealed again through her snorkel and the dolphin repeated its trick. Then EJ held out some fish and the dolphin swam up and took it from her hand. No one would believe this—not that she would be able to tell anyone. EJ swam back to the platform and climbed up. When she turned around, Squirt was there, waiting for her—and for more fish.

"Okay, here are some more," she said, laughing as she threw out some more fish. The dolphin leapt up and out of the water to catch the fish. EJ laughed. "You sure do like these fish!" she cried.

"You can use your agent ID app on your phone to find out about your new partner," C2C suggested.

EJ took a photo of the dolphin and opened the app. Her screen flashed.

AGENT IDENTITY CONFIRMED
MARINE AGENT SQUIRT
FEMALE
AGE: 10
SPECIAL SKILLS: FOREIGN OBJECT
LOCATION
SPECIAL INSTRUCTIONS: REWARD
WITH FISH

"Hey, we're the same age!" cried EJ. "What a team!"

Squirt did a flip in the air. Could she have possibly understood?

Piinngg!

It was EJ's phone.

"It's a message from **SHINE**," said EJ. "At least a message from **SHINE** saying that they have intercepted another message from *SHADOW*."

"What does *SHADOW*'s message say?" asked C2C.

"I'm not sure yet," said EJ. "I don't recognize the code."

EJ stared at the message on the screen, but it didn't seem to make any sense to her.

For the eyes of EJ12 only.

(Message intercepted from SHADOW 14.54. Sent to EJ12 14.55.)

ЗKⴼႦꓭᴇႦ ᴶⵍᗝⵕ ЗKⴼ᙭ⴺ ᗝⵕⵀᴇ

ᘯⴺᴶᴸ ᗝⵕ᙭Ⴆ᙭ⵚⴺⵕᴇ Ⴆᴶⵚⵄⵀᴇᗝ ᴶ᙭ⵀᴇ ᙭ⵍⵚⴺ

Ⴆᴇᴇᴸᴇ ᴇᴶⵍⵂᘖK ⵅⴺ ⵀᴇᴸ

ᘯⴺᴶᴸ ᗝⵕ ⵀⴺⵕᴸ ᴇႦᴇᴇᴸ

ЗKⴼⴺᴇ ⵅᴇᴇᴸ ᴸⵍKᴇⵡ ⵕⵍ ᴸⵍKᴇ ᴇⵅⵕⵕⵄ

ⵕⴺⵅᴇ ᴇᴸⵕⵂ ᴸⵍ ⴼᗝⵕ ⵡⵍⵕႦᴇ

Was it a letter code or was it a picture code? EJ thought it could be either.

"What is that?" asked C2C, looking over EJ's shoulder.

"It's a code, but I am not sure what sort yet," replied EJ. "But Adriana usually uses the same code and just changes it around a bit each time. Which means it should be another mirror code. I am going to try that first."

EJ copied the message and pasted it into the **SHINE** code app on her phone. Then she scrolled through the code app menu until she found "apply mirror." She pressed enter and the screen flashed once. More writing appeared and this time EJ could almost read it. She looked at the first two lines.

HARVEST TWO HALF DONE

BUT DOLPHINS RUINED THE FUN

"Hmmm," she said. "That doesn't look much better, or, wait a moment, does it? They are letters, just really curly ones, almost like coral. That's it!"

"What is?" asked C2C. "I can't see any letters."

"Look closer," said EJ. "The first letter is H, then there's A, then R, V, E,S, T. The first word is HARVEST. Adriana has just made the code harder to read this time by using a curly font."

"Well done, EJ," cried C2C. "What does the rest of the message say?"

EJ keyed in the letters in a clearer font above the first two lines.

HARVEST TWO HALF DONE
HARVEST TWO HALF DONE

BUT DOLPHINS RUINED THE FUN
BUT DOLPHINS RUINED THE FUN

"And now for the next line," EJ said.

```
PESTS STUCK IN NET
PESTS STUCK IN NET

BUT DO NOT FRET
BUT DO NOT FRET
```

"This isn't good," said EJ, "there are dolphins stuck in one of Adriana's nets. There's one more line in the message. I hope it is good news."

It wasn't. EJ looked horrified as she keyed out the last lines.

```
HAVE LEFT THEM ON FLOOR
HAVE LEFT THEM ON FLOOR

WILL STOP TO ADD MORE
WILL STOP TO ADD MORE
```

Now EJ had the whole message. She deleted the curly writing.

> HARVEST TWO HALF DONE
>
> BUT DOLPHINS RUINED THE FUN
>
> PESTS STUCK IN NET
>
> BUT DO NOT FRET
>
> HAVE LEFT THEM ON THE FLOOR
>
> WILL STOP TO ADD MORE

"Oh no!" cried EJ. "We're too late. Adriana has already harvested more coral and she's left dolphins trapped in one of her nets." EJ quickly checked her animal app on her phone. "This is awful: dolphins can't last much longer than thirty minutes without air."

"We need to act fast, EJ," said C2C, climbing on her **SHINE**mobile. "And we will need to split up. I'll search for Adriana. Your phone can give me the location where the message was intercepted. If she stopped to add more nets, she won't have had time to go too far from that point. I should be able to catch her. Squirt will be able to find the sunken net. She is trained to locate any new objects on the ocean floor. You need to get to those dolphins fast. Good luck, EJ12. I hope we both make it in time."

"We have to, C2C," cried EJ, as she ran for her **SHINE**mobile, taking a bucket of fish and stowing it under her seat. "We just have to!"

Chapter •8

EJ looked at Squirt. Squirt looked at EJ.

"Let's go," EJ said, pressing the Search button on the dolphin trainer. Another high-pitched tone sounded. That was Squirt's command to begin her search and the dolphin took off immediately.

EJ jumped on her **SHINE**mobile and took off after Squirt, thumping over the waves as Squirt dived in and out of them. Then EJ noticed that Squirt was spending less time jumping and more and more time swimming in the water.

Is she picking up something? Are we close?

wondered EJ. *I need to be able to follow Squirt.* She checked the time. It was twelve minutes since Adriana had sent the message. EJ had to get to those trapped dolphins quickly. She pressed the S button on the **SHINE**mobile and waited while a shield came over the top of her and the skis folded up underneath. ***SHINE**mobile 3* had converted to sub mode and EJ12 steered it downward, following Squirt as the dolphin dived deeper and deeper.

It was getting darker. The sun's rays were weaker this far down and it was harder to see. EJ switched on ***SHINE**mobile 3*'s headlights and powered through the water past schools of fish. As she sped along after Squirt, EJ noticed that there were fewer and fewer fish and the water was growing murkier.

EJ was suspicious. Keeping one hand on the steering wheel, she activated her test flask charm and inserted it into the robotic aqua-arm cabinet and shut the watertight door. She switched the arm on and it slowly moved, extending outside the sub. Once outside, the flask took in water. EJ pressed the button again and the arm retracted with the flask.

Even as she took the flask back out of the cabinet she could see that the water was extremely cloudy with streaks of black through it. EJ pressed the small button on the neck of the flask. The results would be sent to her phone. As she waited for them, she suddenly realized that she could no longer see Squirt. Just as EJ began to worry, she saw the dolphin coming down from the surface.

She must have gone up for air, thought EJ. *She can, unlike the poor dolphins trapped in Adriana's nets.*

Squirt swam forward and EJ followed closely behind.

Piinngg!

WATER TEST RESULT
REQUESTED BY AGENT EJ12
WATER STATUS: POLLUTED
SUSPECT INDUSTRIAL ACTIVITY
TRACES OF OILS

Oil? From the A-Sub perhaps? thought EJ. *At least it is only a trace.*

EJ knew the real problem was the pollution and the industrial activity that caused it and as she looked up away from her phone and out the window she could see exactly what that activity had done. Horrified, EJ saw that they had come to a part of the reef that had been completely destroyed. There were broken and crushed bits of coral and shredded seaweed. A solitary zebra fish darted to and fro as if looking for its home.

EJ had found Adriana's harvest area but too late. She hoped, however, that she could still save the dolphins.

"Adriana has been here so the net must be close," she said to herself. "Come on, Squirt, where is it?"

Squirt had gone back up for air but was now swimming down again, all the time clicking. EJ could hear the dolphin through a speaker that went outside the sub. It was the clicking noises that enabled the dolphin to find things and EJ was amazed how the dolphin moved so quickly through the dark water. Then, all of a sudden, as Squirt swam through the destroyed reef, her clicking stopped and was replaced by a short, piercing whistle. Then EJ heard new noises, more distressed sounding than Squirt's. Squirt started to make buzzing noises, blowing bubbles furiously and flapping her tail.

EJ saw why. Squirt had found the broken net and tangled up inside it were two bottlenose dolphins, thrashing to get out, making frantic buzzing, whistling noises as they did. EJ couldn't believe it. Adriana had just left the dolphins there to die. EJ had no time to lose if she was to save them.

Slowly she drove the sub close to the net. She checked the dashboard, activated the robotic aqua-arm and switched the sub on to auto-hover. Using a joystick to guide the robotic arm, EJ tried to pull the net away from the trapped dolphins.

"Come on, come on," she urged herself, but the net was too tangled.

I'm going to have to cut them free, thought EJ, and she pressed another button on the sub's dashboard. Another arm extended from the side of the sub. This one had a cutting saw on its end. Carefully, knowing that one wrong move could cut a dolphin and not the net, EJ used the grip arm to hold a piece of net up and the cutter to tear it. The two trapped dolphins stopped thrashing around, as if they knew EJ was trying to help them.

"One more slice and I should have cut away enough net to pull it free," EJ told herself. "Hang in there guys, hang in there!"

EJ grabbed another piece of net and raised it as high as the robotic arm would let her. She then pulled the cutting device down, ripping through the net. With the gripping arm still holding the net, she then put the sub into reverse. With a jolt, the net lurched backward and the two dolphins fell out. They were free. In a frenzy, they shot up through the water to the surface.

Squirt and EJ followed and Squirt seemed to be pushing the dolphins up, as if she were helping them get to the surface. Would they make it in time?

When EJ surfaced, she was relieved to see the

two dolphins opening and closing their blowholes—they were sucking in air and blowing it out again. They looked calmer now that they could breathe.

EJ converted *SHINEmobile 3* to jet ski mode and reached under the seat for the fish.

"Good job, Squirt," said EJ, throwing the dolphin some fish. "That was close. Let's hope C2C has been just as successful." She threw out some more fish, and the two recovering dolphins gobbled some down too.

EJ checked her phone, but there was no message from C2C. She tried to call her, but there was no answer. That was strange and definitely not good. Had C2C found Adriana—or had Adriana found C2C first?

Piinngg!

Another message. EJ just had a feeling that it wouldn't be good news.

Chapter •9

(Message intercepted from SHADOW
12.26. Sent to EJ12 12.27.)

SEE THE UNDER STAIRS SOMETHING FOUND

THREE HUNDRED FOR ME WITH IT TAKE MANY

EJ looked at it. It was quite a short code and it
seemed to be the same mirror code in the same
crazy font as last time. EJ smiled to herself. *Adriana
is getting a bit lazy. This won't take long at all.*

She again pasted the message into the code app and applied the mirror app to each line. She keyed in what she saw in a font that was easier to read.

SEA THE UNDER SHINY SOMETHING FOUND

SEA THE UNDER SHINY SOMETHING FOUND

THREE HARVEST FOR ME WITH IT TAKE WILL

THREE HARVEST FOR ME WITH IT TAKE WILL

Hmmm, I take that back, thought EJ, looking at what she had just keyed. *Adriana must have changed the code because this doesn't make sense.*

SEA THE UNDER SHINY SOMETHING FOUND
THREE HARVEST FOR ME WITH IT TAKE WILL

At least it didn't make sense if you read it normally, left to right. But no one thought Adriana was normal. EJ rekeyed the text right to left.

FOUND SOMETHING SHINY UNDER THE SEA
WILL TAKE IT WITH ME FOR HARVEST THREE

Something shiny, that's got to be a **SHINE** *agent—C2C!* thought EJ. *Adriana has captured C2C and is taking her along to her next harvest area. We will have to hurry. We can't let Adriana start another harvest.*

"Squirt," said EJ, turning to her dolphin buddy, "I think we have another rescue mission."

Adriana's A-Sub might be hard to find in the water but C2C's sub wasn't—if the A-Sub was holding the other agent's **SHINE**mobile, Squirt should be able to find them.

A light on EJ's dashboard started to flash. EJ reconnected her phone and her screen flashed as well.

```
C2C SHINEMOBILE
HOMING DEVICE ACTIVATED
TRACK ON SUB RADAR
```

"Yes," shouted EJ. "C2C has activated the homing device on her sub. Looks like you are going to have some help. Come on, Squirt!"

EJ pressed the S button and the shield came up as *SHINEmobile 3* went into sub mode and EJ once again headed deep down into the water.

EJ was steering her way through the last of what had been a long series of underwater canyons when the light on her dashboard started to flash faster, just as Squirt started to flap her tail and make her distressed buzzing noises. EJ had to be close.

She reversed back into the reef, then turned off the engine and waited: if it was the A-Sub, she didn't want to be caught like C2C. In the distance, she could see a large submarine, long and black with windows all the way around the front half of the boat, moving through the water. As it came closer, she could see the letters on the side: A-SUB. As the vessel came closer still, she could make out someone standing at the front looking out of the windows. It was a woman with jet-black hair swept up in a big beehive-like but messy bun, and black, thick, thick glasses. It was Adriana on the A-Sub, the Adriana Submarine. *Trust Adriana to name her submarine after herself*. And then EJ saw the thing that was different about the A-Sub: underneath, on the submarine's bottom, were two sets of poles and between each of them hung a giant net made of heavy chains. One net was closed and full of coral and one was open.

"That's how she harvests the coral," said EJ to herself. "The A-Sub drags the net along the bottom of the seabed and it pulls along the coral with it. No wonder it makes such a mess; it just rips out everything! And then Adriana pulls up the net and takes her precious black coral."

Then, suddenly, there were clanking noises and the A-Sub began to turn and, as it did, EJ could see C2C's **SHINE**mobile attached to the side, held in a giant clamp. Adriana had captured it. Then the nets underneath the A-Sub started to move. At the same time, from the top of the sub, a pole with a huge searchlight attached to the end began to extend into the water. EJ held her breath. The bright light was coming closer and closer. Had she found Adriana or had Adriana found her?

Adriana must be preparing for the next coral harvesting, thought EJ. *I can't let that happen. But if I take* **SHINE**mobile 3 *closer I'll be captured just like C2C.* EJ swallowed and her mouth felt dry. *There's nothing for it. I will have to swim.*

Then in her mind, she heard Nema's voice again. "You're not still afraid of the deep end, are you? Only little kids are afraid of the deep end. Babies."

"Well, are you?" said EJ to herself. She looked out the sub's window at the water, then she looked at the A-Sub and Adriana's haul of coral. She bit her lip. Then she looked out the window and saw Squirt, who seemed to be looking at her, waiting. "No, I am not," she said out loud, "but I'm glad I have a dive buddy."

"Okay, okay, I'm coming," she said, laughing. She wasn't scared at all, she had just forgotten to tell herself that. She should actually thank Nema. Well, maybe not.

EJ switched the *SHINEmobile 3* sub to auto-hover and activated the homing device. She then sent a text to A1. **SHINE** would now know exactly where to come to find her sub. Then EJ took out the scuba gear from behind her seat, and pulled on her tank, flippers and mask. Taking a deep breath, she moved to the back and opened the door to the escape hatch. Submarines had hatches to allow divers to leave and enter a submarine while it was under the water. The divers first entered a small, sealed chamber that separated the rest of the sub from the sea. Once the diver was in that chamber, she could then open the next door and enter the ocean. EJ closed the first door and then opened the next one. She was in the water. She closed the door behind her and clicked her dive shoes together and waited for them to convert to flippers. She then swam away from her sub. Seconds later, and unknown to EJ, the A-Sub's searchlight swept over *SHINEmobile 3.*

Chapter • 10

Bubbles streamed behind EJ as she glided slowly through the water. Squirt swam next to her, clicking and whistling. The A-Sub's searchlight kept swinging around and EJ kept her eyes firmly on Adriana, who was standing at the window squinting, as she watched out through the water. The A-Sub seemed to turn back toward EJ.

Uh-oh, thought EJ, *Adriana's bound to see me and if she does, I'm done for. I need somewhere to hide. And quick.*

And then, as if on cue, a school of large fish

swam by, large black fish, each one as big as both of EJ's hands, with flashes of yellow and deep purple on their tails. There were scores of them and, as they swam past EJ, everything seemed to go black for a moment. She couldn't see anything except fish. And that gave EJ an idea on how she might make it to the top of the A-Sub without being seen by Adriana.

Can I use the fish to hide me? wondered EJ. *My wetsuit is almost exactly the same color as their scales and if I can just get enough of them to keep swimming with me, it just might work.*

EJ took off her fish charm and twisted it. She was holding a small bottle with a lid like a saltshaker. There was a label.

Reef Feed

Shake and stand back

The bottle held fish food. EJ shook the lid and a cloud of tiny particles flooded out of the bottle and floated in the water. EJ waited and watched. No fish. *Maybe that wasn't enough?* she thought. She shook out more particles. That did it. In seconds the school of large black fish returned, but they were not alone. Hundreds of other fish, large and small, rushed to eat the reef feed, all frantically pushing each other to get at it. And in the middle of the mass of tussling fish was EJ.

The commotion did not go unnoticed by Adriana. Through the mass of fish, EJ could just make out Adriana peering over in her direction. Did that mean Adriana could also see her? The A-Sub's spotlight swept over EJ and the fish. EJ fed out more fish food and more fish came. Just when EJ was convinced she had been discovered, she saw Adriana shrug her shoulders and look away.

Phew, thought EJ. *That was close. If I can just keep swimming and feeding them, these fish will keep hiding me and I should be able to make it to the top of the A-Sub and over to C2C's* **SHINE***mobile.*

It worked like a charm. EJ kept releasing fish food and hundreds of fish kept flocking around her as she swam closer and closer to the A-Sub. When she reached the top of the vessel, she stopped sprinkling the reef feed and slowly, the fish drifted away. EJ hovered above the A-sub and then saw C2C's **SHINE**mobile. She slowly swam down to it and peered in the window. C2C's face smiled out at her. EJ gave her the thumbs-up and C2C smiled again, also giving the thumbs-up. C2C then pointed upward and wrote in the condensation on her window.

EJ admired C2C's handwriting—and the fact that she was writing backward—but there was no time for that now. She gave C2C the thumbs-up again and swam back up to the top of the A-Sub. EJ pulled herself along the top until she came to a door with a large metal wheel, the A-Sub's escape hatch. She pulled hard to twist the wheel lock. It didn't budge. EJ tried again and this time she felt it give a little. She pulled again with both arms straining on the wheel and both legs pushing on the sub's roof. Finally, with a last heave, she felt the wheel turn. She spun the wheel once around and pulled the door open, then slid into the small chamber as the water rushed in. Once inside, EJ tightly turned the wheel lock on the other side of the door and pressed a button on the wall next to a light that flashed red. As she did, the water was pumped out and another light flashed green. The cabin was sealed and airtight. EJ took off her air tank and opened the next hatch below, dropping into the submarine cabin. She clicked her flippers and they converted to dive shoes.

She had made it past the searchlight, through

the deep water, had checked that C2C was all right and that gotten into the submarine. EJ was feeling pretty proud of herself. Now all she had to do was find Adriana and figure out a way to stop her. No problem. EJ moved across to open the door in front of her. She hoped it would lead her to Adriana—just not quite as fast as it did.

"Well, well, who might this be? Another Shiny friend from under the sea!"

It was Adriana.

"So, we meet again, EJ12. Will you never learn? Yes, that's right, it's me, I told you I'd return."

Chapter •11

Adriana had led EJ out to the observation room of the submarine. In the middle of the deck was a large tank filled with what EJ instantly recognized as live black coral. Brilliantly colored coral but with a jet-black skeleton.

"Isn't it beautiful?" asked Adriana. "So fine, so fragile, so valuable."

"It's more beautiful in the sea," said EJ.

"Well, maybe, but it's no good there. You can't use it to make beautiful jewelry," replied Adriana, stroking the large black pendant that hung around her neck. "And my coral is perfect for jewelry. The tests of my first harvest show it to be of the highest quality. You have no idea how much money *SHADOW* and I can make from selling my coral."

"Except it's not your coral."

"It is now," said Adriana, smiling smugly.

"But you can't just take it," cried EJ. "And your harvesting collects the rest of the reef as well."

"But I just did take it," said Adriana. "And anyway, I throw back all other stuff."

"But it's too late then, it's destroyed."

"Oh I suppose that's a pity," sighed Adriana. "But the jewelry is so pretty and I do like pretty things." Adriana's squinty eyes glared meanly at EJ over the top of her thick black glasses. "But now, I'm bored with talking to you, EJ Nothing," she said, her voice hardening. "In fact, I am tired of you always trying to ruin my projects, you little goody-goody. You're as bad as my sister. Actually, shall I tell you a little secret about your precious A1?"

"No!" shouted EJ. "You shouldn't tell other people's secrets."

"Why not? I was never very good at keeping secrets," said Adriana.

"Well you should get better," said EJ.

"Oh should I now?" snapped Adriana. "Do you really think that you can tell me what to do, EJ-worrywart-12?" Adriana cackled. "*You* can't stop me."

"Yes I can. We can. I have alerted A1 to our location and she and a team of **SHINE** agents will be here at any moment."

Adriana stopped cackling, her smile fell away and she was completely still for a moment. "Well, not that I wouldn't love a family reunion…"

And with that, Adriana pressed her pendant. The floor underneath her opened and she dropped down to a lower deck of the submarine. EJ rushed over, but the floor closed up again before she could get across the room. There was a loud, clanking noise as if something was moving from underneath the deck. Then a voice boomed over a speaker somewhere in the observation room.

"Thanks for dropping in, EJ. Do give my worst to

A1, but I really can't stay. You know how it is. I win, you lose."

EJ rushed to the window to see that Adriana was making her escape in a small black mini sub.

"I don't think so, Adriana. You're not getting away this time," said EJ12, as she rushed to the A-Sub's control panel.

The control panel was enormous. There were buttons, levers, dials and flashing lights everywhere, but EJ wasn't one of **SHINE**'s leading agents for nothing. She knew exactly what she was looking for as she scanned the panel. First she flicked an audio switch and spoke into a handset.

"C2C, do you copy?" said EJ into the radio.

"I copy, EJ," replied C2C. "I am so pleased to hear your voice."

"I'm going to pull the release lever for the robotic clamp that's holding your **SHINE**mobile. Hold on."

"Check," said C2C.

EJ scanned across the board and then pulled a lever on the right. "C2C, did that work?"

"No, I think that one controls the net. Try another one."

EJ pulled the next lever. She heard another clanking sound from the back of the A-Sub.

"That was it. Well done. EJ, my sub's oxygen levels are low so I need to surface. Will you be okay?"

"Oh yes," said EJ, smiling. "I have everything under control. I'm now in pursuit of Adriana." EJ was going to enjoy this. Adriana had escaped from her last time and there was no way EJ12 would let that happen again.

With C2C's **SHINE**mobile now safely clear, EJ switched the engine to turbo and the A-Sub surged forward, racing through the water. EJ could see Adriana's mini sub just ahead. Its engines were no match for the A-Sub's powerful ones and she gained on Adriana quickly. She then pulled the net lever again and waited. As she drew in closer to the mini sub, EJ pulled the A-Sub up higher in the water and moved the net lever down.

"Just a little farther, just a little farther," she said. Adriana's mini sub was now directly in front of the A-Sub's net. If EJ could just get close enough, she would be able to activate the net.

"Perfect," said EJ, as she pushed the button to open the net. The net hovered over the mini sub.

EJ pushed the button to close the net. "Gotcha," she said, and she began to bring both the A-Sub and the now entangled mini sub up to the surface. EJ could see a very cross Adriana looking up at her.

Piinngg!

There was a message from **SHINE** on EJ's phone.

SUB LOCATION RECEIVED.
BACKUP TEAM ON ITS WAY.
ETA THREE MINUTES.
CONFIRM STATUS.

EJ12 smiled as she sent her reply.

ADRIANA IS A LITTLE UPSET.
FINALLY CAUGHT IN HER
OWN NET.
EJI2 ☺

Chapter •12

EJ climbed out through the escape hatch and stood on top of the A-Sub, looking up at the sky and breathing in the fresh air. The underwater world was amazing, but it was nice to be back in more familiar territory. She smiled as she looked out and saw a large boat, with the two **SHINE** mobiles being towed behind, coming toward her. A1, C2C and F15H were standing on its deck. A1 beamed at EJ as the boat drew in alongside the A-Sub.

"Well done, EJ12," A1 cried. "Your best mission yet, I think. Not only have you stopped the coral harvest, you rescued C2C, captured the A-Sub and, last but certainly not least, you have captured Adriana."

"Thank you, A1," said EJ, blushing. "Adriana is in the mini sub. I don't think she will be very pleased to see you."

"Neither do I," said A1. "Agent F15H will make sure Adriana is taken away. We will put her to work, under guard, in the **SHINE** laboratories. She can develop some ways to fix the reef she has destroyed. C2C will take care of the A-Sub, and EJ, we need to get you back home. You must be tired."

EJ groaned. Sometimes A1 was just a little bit too much like her mom.

"Jump aboard, EJ. It's time to go home. Mission accomplished."

They slowly navigated the boat over the reef but, as they hit open seas, the captain opened up the engine and the boat almost flew across the water. It was fantastic, but EJ kept looking out hopefully across the sea.

"Looking for something, EJ12?" A1 asked.

"I was just hoping to say good-bye to Squirt," said EJ a little sadly, still looking out to sea. Things had gotten so busy that she hadn't noticed the dolphin swimming off.

"Well, I think you could probably use your charm one more time," said A1. "After all, technically, you are still on a mission."

EJ jumped up and almost hugged A1 before stopping, thinking that wasn't particularly secret agent-like. Instead, she took out her dolphin charm, twisted it and pressed the Return button.

"Maybe you would like to wait in the water for her," called the captain. "We can pull you along on the side with a rope—dolphins love swimming behind boats and you can swim together."

The boat slowed down and EJ jumped in and grabbed hold of the rope. As the boat sped up again, she felt the rush as she was swept along through the waves. It was exhilarating.

"Look behind you," shouted A1.

EJ turned her head. At first she could only see the foam from the boat, but then she glimpsed a fin. She shrieked with excitement as Squirt rose out of the water and then dived down right next to her. As EJ was pulled through the water, Squirt swam alongside her, diving in and out of the wake. When EJ put her head under the water, she could hear the dolphin's clicks and whistles. There was no buzzing now that all was well. After what seemed only minutes but what A1 assured her was much, much longer, EJ reluctantly climbed back into the boat. She looked out to sea as Squirt did one final leap into the air before swimming away. EJ could have sworn the dolphin was looking right at her, almost smiling.

Maybe she was.

Chapter • 13

Back at home, it was the day of the swim meet. It was about twenty seconds before the start of the girls' under-twelve freestyle relay race.

The meet official was starting the race. "On your marks. Get set. Go!"

Nema was the first swimmer. She sprang off the blocks at the other end of the pool and powered down the lane toward where Emma and Hannah were waiting for their turns to swim. Nema was easily coming first in her leg. The moment she touched the edge of the pool, Hannah dived in. She set off strongly but was slowly being overtaken by a girl in lane four.

"Come on, Han," yelled Emma, who was now on the block Hannah had just dived off. She would be the last swimmer.

Nema climbed out of the pool beside her. As soon as Nema had her breath back, she shouted, "Go, Hannah! You can do it!"

Emma looked at Nema, surprised. *That was nice of her,* she thought. Then they both yelled at the same time, "Go, Hannah!"

Up at the other end of the pool, Isi for once wasn't yelling and jumping up and down. She was leaning forward, ready to dive in.

Hannah slapped the end of the pool, finishing second in her leg but only just. Isi dived off the blocks for the third leg.

Emma stopped shouting and prepared herself for her swim. She shook her legs and looked down into the deep water, smiling. The only thing she was worried about now was not being able to swim fast enough.

Isi raced up the length of the pool and stretched to touch the end in second place. Emma dived in.

"Go, Em, go, Em, go, Em!" chanted all three girls who had run down to the finishing end to wait for her. Each time Emma came up for air she could hear them screaming her name.

She kept kicking as hard as she could; she knew she could catch the girl just in front. As she turned to breathe with only five meters to go, Emma took her final breath of the race. She put her head down and willed her arms to go faster, stronger.

Emma and the girl in lane four were neck and neck. At two meters, Emma took one final stroke and propelled herself to the edge. She touched. Just in front.

The girls had won the relay! The crowd cheered loudly. It had been the closest race of the meet. Emma climbed out of the pool and was immediately mobbed by the other girls. Isi squeezed her so hard, she could hardly breathe.

A beaming Ms. Tenga came up and congratulated the girls. She turned to Emma. "Congratulations, Emma," she whispered. "On both victories."

Emma grinned.

It was the end of the swim meet. All the girls were proudly wearing their blue ribbons and Isi and Hannah had gone to ask Ms. Tenga if they were allowed in the dive pool, leaving Emma and Nema alone together. Nema looked a bit uncomfortable, and then turned slightly toward Emma.

"I'm sorry I told everyone your secret," whispered Nema.

Emma did a double take. "Pardon?" she said.

"I'm sorry I made fun of you. I shouldn't have done that," Nema said.

Emma was surprised but grateful. "Thanks," she said. "Anyway, I'm not afraid of deep water anymore, you know."

"I didn't think so," said Nema. "You're not scared of *anything* are you, Emma?"

Emma did another double take. *Is that what Nema thinks?*

Isi bounded up to them.

"We can! We can! Ms. Tenga said we can do cannonballs! Come on!" she cried, as Hannah came up behind her. "But let's do a *team* cannonball into the diving pool!"

The four girls stood on the edge of the pool.

"Let's hold hands and all jump together," yelled Isi, grabbing Hannah's hand.

Hannah grabbed Emma's hand and Emma looked at Nema. Then Emma put her hand out and smiled. Nema smiled back and took Emma's hand and, together, the whole team jumped out and up in the air over the deep end.

Emma was in over her head—and loving it!

With, she thought to herself, *only a little help from EJ12*!

Emma Jacks and EJ12 return in

BOOK 8
DRAMA QUEEN

Collect them all!

HOT & COLD

JUMP START

IN THE DARK

ROCKY ROAD

CHOC SHOCK

ON THE BALL

MAKING WAVES

DRAMA QUEEN